CRASH IN THE WILDERNESS

CRASH IN THE WILDERNESS

Susan Black

Illustrated by Thomas Buchs

RAINTREE PUBLISHERS
Milwaukee • Toronto • Melbourne • London

Copyright © 1980, Raintree Publishers Inc.

All rights reserved. No part of this book may be reproduced or utilized in any form or by any means, electronic or mechanical, including photocopying, recording, or by any information storage and retrieval system, without permission in writing from the Publisher. Inquiries should be addressed to Raintree Publishers Inc., 205 West Highland Avenue, Milwaukee, Wisconsin 53203.

Library of Congress Number: 79-21852

2 3 4 5 6 7 8 9 0 84 83 82 81

Printed and bound in the United States of America.

Library of Congress Cataloging in Publication Data

Black, Susan.
  Crash in the wilderness.

  SUMMARY: Relates the 10-mile journey to safety of the sole survivor of a plane crash in the Sierra Nevada Mountains.
    1.   Survival (after airplane accidents, shipwrecks, etc.) — Juvenile literature.
  2.   Aeronautics — California — Accidents — 1976 — Juvenile literature. 3.   Elder, Lauren — Juvenile literature. [1.   Survival] I. Buchs, Thomas.
II. Title.
TL553.9.B54   979.4'86'050924 [B]   79-21852
ISBN 0-8172-1553-0 lib. bdg.

CONTENTS

CHAPTER 1

The Sight of Your Life

When she woke up early that April morning, the first thing twenty-nine year old Lauren Elder saw was the crisp, clear blue of the California sky. She had no plans today, no important work to do. She wondered how she would pass the long spring day that stretched ahead of her. Lauren had no way of knowing that within hours she would be in a desperate struggle between life and death.

But right now, the biggest challenge Lauren faced was getting out of bed. She winced when her feet touched the cold hardwood floor, and ran into the kitchen to make coffee. "If only I could fly," she grumbled, hopping from one foot to the other as she waited for the water to boil. "Then my feet would never have to touch the ground!"

As the kettle began its slow whistle, Lauren remembered something that made her laugh out loud. She ran to the phone and quickly dialed her friend Jay Fuller's number. He ran a small veterinary clinic in Oakland. But whenever he got the chance he would take off to go sailing, backpacking, or flying. A few days ago he had told her about his plans for a flight to Death Valley, and had invited her to go along. Today it sounded like a great idea, and she hoped that she wasn't too late.

"Dr. Fuller," Jay's voice answered the phone, and Lauren sighed, pleased.

"Jay, it's Lauren. Are you still going up in the plane today? I'd like to go along if it's still okay!"

"No problem," Jay laughed. "Jean's going too, and we're just about to leave. We'll come by and pick you up in about twenty minutes." He hung up before she could say anything more, and Lauren grinned at the phone. Jay was not one to waste words.

Lauren decided to dress up for the trip and make it a really special day. Pulling on her favorite leather boots, she thought how much better it would be to sketch valleys and waterfalls as she flew above them, instead of just painting them from imagination in her studio. Gazing at herself in the mirror, she was pleased with the look of the skirt, the vest, and especially the smile. "It's about time I had some adventure," she thought.

Outside, a car horn honked, and Lauren

grabbed her camera and her sketchpad. She didn't want to keep her friends waiting, so she decided not to search in her closet for a coat. She probably wouldn't need one anyway. Who needs to keep warm in a desert?

When they reached the airport, Jay went to rent the Cessna 182 plane, while Lauren and Jean loaded it with their cameras, sandwiches, and a couple of cartons of beer. They laughed as Lauren pulled out a tissue and wiped the dust from the windshield.

"Good idea," Jay said, walking towards them with maps and a clipboard.

"Did you register our flight plan?" Lauren asked. Her father was a pilot, and she was famil-

iar with some of the regulations. To her surprise, Jay shook his head.

"It's not important," he said, tossing his windbreaker into the plane and climbing into the pilot's seat. "This is just a short trip." He seemed to know what he was doing, so Lauren didn't say anything.

As she watched Jean climb into the seat next to him, Lauren had a sudden, uncomfortable feeling. Something way in the back of her head seemed to be saying: DON'T GO.

"Hey, what's wrong?" Jean was looking at her from the window where she sat, cheerful and full of energy. Lauren pushed the strange feeling out of her mind. Then she pulled herself in behind Jean, closing the door after her.

"Everything's great!" she shouted over the sound of the engines as the Cessna rolled down the runway. Within moments they were in the air, high above Oakland, and flying towards the nearby Central valley. Jay looked at his watch and smiled with pleasure.

"Right on schedule!" he said. It was twelve o'clock noon, and sunlight poured through the windows as they made their way across the farm land below. Lauren liked the checkerboard look of the fields. She had not imagined that the world would look so peaceful from up above, and she

was thrilled when she saw the foothills of the mountains rise up in the distance.

Suddenly a strong gust of wind rocked the plane, and Lauren's sketching pencils fell to the floor. She saw that Jay and Jean were not concerned, and decided not to worry about the wind. Flying in a small plane would just take some getting used to.

"We're coming into the Sierra mountains now," Jay announced. Lauren looked up from her sketchpad to see that they were flying over the foothills she had seen in the distance only a short time ago. Now she saw that they grew into a magnificent mountain wilderness up ahead. She took her camera from the back of the plane and began to take pictures of the incredible rock formations and timberlands below. At times the small plane seemed to fly so close to the mountain peaks that Lauren felt she could reach out

and touch them. She wondered how she would paint them when she got back, they were so large and powerful.

Lauren lowered her camera from the window, and was astonished to realize that they were now surrounded on all sides by jagged mountain peaks. The valleys and foothills were far behind them, and they seemed to be drifting in a world of twisted rock.

"Look just up ahead," Jay said, pointing out a mountain range which spanned the horizon in front of them. "We're going to fly through that pass up ahead. When we do, get ready for the sight of your life. Death Valley is just over that range."

Lauren flipped to a blank page on her pad and began to draw the stunning view. Her heart was racing with excitement. The little plane was coming closer and closer to the narrow mountain pass Jay had pointed out. The blue sky began to disappear behind the rocky peaks.

"Hang on!" Jay cautioned. "Get ready for a sharp drop when the air currents change!" Lauren fumbled with her seatbelt, but looked up sharply when she heard Jean's frightened gasp. All she could see through the windshield was a vast wall of stone. Then there was a crash and the noise of scraping and crunching in her ears. A moment later, everything was dark and silent.

CHAPTER 2

I'm Not Going to Die

Opening her eyes, Lauren felt that the world must have turned upside down. Her body ached, and there was a sharp pain in her leg. She looked down to see a deep gash bleeding just above her knee. There was a throbbing in her arm. She looked up and saw Jay in the front seat, dazed, with blood all over his face from a cut above the eye. Jean was slumped over in her seat, unconscious.

"Quick, Jay," Lauren shouted. "Help me get Jean out of the plane." Together they dragged Jean from the cockpit, gasping with each painful step. The thin mountain air made even the slightest movement difficult. As soon as they had placed Jean securely on the rocks they sank down next to her in exhaustion.

"God, how stupid." Jay moaned, gazing at the wreckage of the plane. They had crashed into the mountain face, only fifteen feet below the crest. The left wingtip of the plane was buried in the

mountain, and the tail section was cracked open. Broken bottles of beer were scattered all over the rocks, and gas was dripping steadily from underneath the wing. Lauren looked at Jay in confusion.

"What happened?" she asked, still not used to the sound of her own voice in this mountain wilderness.

"I tried to make it through the mountain pass, but I wasn't prepared for the downdraft. It was just too strong."

Lauren could hear the misery in Jay's voice. "Don't think about it now," she told him. "Let's just try to figure out what we're going to do."

Jay began to climb slowly around to the back of the plane, each step heavy and painful. Lauren noticed the dripping gas and had a sudden, terrible thought.

"Jay! There's gas leaking from the wing!" she shouted. "The plane might explode!"

"It won't," he answered, and Lauren felt relieved. Jay knew the answers, Jay knew what to do. She tried to ignore the strange, trembling sound in his voice. He was in the cockpit of the plane now, calling for help over the radio. Lauren heard his cries of "Mayday!" and waited for a response, but there was only silence. Jay clicked the radio off. His face was blank as he crawled over the rocks to her and Jean.

"I can't keep her still," Lauren said. She was

holding on the shoulder straps of Jean's overalls.
But Jean, though unconscious, was moaning and
struggling against her. Every time she moved,
she would slip a little way down the rocks and pull
Lauren with her. Jay sat next to her and tried to
help Lauren keep her steady. They tried to move
her back into the plane, thinking she would be
safer there. But they didn't have the strength to
carry her. She had already slipped too far down
the rocky mountainside.

"We've got to keep her warm," Jay said. Lauren
saw that Jean had lost her sandals in the crash.
Quickly she took her own socks off and put them
on Jean's feet. As she zipped her boots back on,
Lauren saw that Jay was bent over, hugging his
stomach in pain. She knew that his injuries were
much worse than she had first thought.

"You hold on to Jean," she said. "I'm going to
try the radio again. Just tell me what to do." She
climbed into the plane and followed Jay's instruc-

tions, but still nothing happened. Glancing at the clock next to the radio, she saw that the face was cracked and the hands were frozen at 2:15 P.M. The numbers burned themselves into her memory. Lauren looked at the sky and knew that time was the most important thing now. She guessed that it was about three o'clock. They had three more hours of sunlight left, maybe four. Lauren trembled at the thought of spending the cold night on the mountaintop.

"I've turned on the emergency radio beacon in the tail," Jay called to her. "It will send out a constant signal." Lauren began to feel a glimmer of hope. She asked Jay if he thought a search party would be sent soon.

"Not today, it's too late," he answered. Lauren's heart sank. She looked up at the top of the crest, and decided to climb to it. She made her way up the fifteen feet of rock at a steady pace, and peered over the edge. What she saw made her reel.

Below her, the side of the mountain plunged almost straight down thousands of feet to the desert valley below. Down there were houses, ranches, people who could help. Lauren decided to make the climb herself, and scrambled back to the plane to get her backpack and her knife. She thought she might be able to make it to the desert before dark.

Returning to the crest, Lauren saw that she would have to dig her hands and feet into the icy crust of the mountain face and edge her way down slowly. She tried this, making sure not to strain her hurt arm. When she had gone about six feet she looked up to view her progress, and was terrified at what she saw. The mountain curved like the inside of a cup. One wrong move would hurtle her through the air for hundreds of feet before the hard icy surface broke her fall. The climb was much too steep and dangerous. Lauren took a deep breath and inched her way back up to the top. When she finally made it back to the plane, she saw Jay sitting in the same, hunched-over position. Jean was nowhere in sight. She must have fallen off the ledge, Lauren thought. There was nothing they could do for her now.

It was time to face facts. She and Jay would have to spend the night on the mountain. And they would have to find some way of staying warm. "I am not going to die!" Lauren thought to herself, fighting back the tears.

Together she and Jay searched the rocks for everything they could find that would burn. There were bits of paper and wood, but neither of them had any matches. Jay tore a piece of paper from a brown bag and wet it with gas from the leaking tank.

19

"Try the cigarette lighter on this," he said. Lauren found the button on the control board, and stuck the paper into it when it was red and glowing. They cheered when it burst into flame, and huddled next to the tiny fire they lit with it. Too soon, the flames began to die. They realized that they would have to keep it going with gasoline.

Lauren scrambled underneath the plane, filling empty beer bottles with fuel from the leaking engine. She handed the bottles to Jay one by one, and in turn he fed the fire. They kept the fire going this way until long after darkness fell. Lauren guessed that it was about two o'clock in the morning when she saw the fire growing dim. She rushed over and poured gas on the flame while Jay tried to shield it from the wind. But it was too late. They were surrounded by darkness and bitter cold.

CHAPTER 3

Alone

The cold air bit into her lungs. Lauren shivered miserably. She knew that she and Jay would not live through the hours of darkness that stretched ahead unless they found a way to keep warm. They would have to move back into the plane, of course. But would that be enough? Lauren noticed that the rocks around the fire had absorbed the heat. She realized that they would keep the inside of the plane warm.

"Jay," she called, "we've got to put as many rocks as we can into the tail of the plane! There'll be room for both of us there, and we can stay warm." Jay made no answer, so Lauren tried again. "If we load it full of rocks, do you think it will tip over?" This time he spoke. But his voice sounded a million miles away in the darkness.

"It's OK," he said, but that was all. His tone told Lauren that he would not be joining her in the work. The pain of his injuries and of losing Jean had been too much for him. Lauren realized that he had finally given up.

Lauren, unable to see the stones in the darkness, searched for them with her hands. She stuffed some small ones into her pockets, and began to drag the larger ones into the plane. The work was painfully hard. Many times she had to stop to catch her breath. Her hands were burned and oily, and her fingernails broken and bloody. But she was able to make herself a warm little nest that was protected from the wind outside. She curled up and rested for a while, feeling the exhaustion wash over her.

Later, she went back out into the night to find more rocks to bring to the plane. Her strength seemed to be gone, though, and lugging the rocks seemed almost impossible. Desperately, she called to Jay from the baggage door of the plane.

"Will you *please* hand me some rocks, Jay? There are some right near you." His voice snapped back at her: "No." It sent a shiver up her spine.

Lauren could barely make out his form in the darkness. Crouching on a rock, he rose slowly, and stumbled over to the plane. The walls shook as he climbed in, and Lauren sighed deeply. At least he wasn't giving up altogether.

It seemed to take Lauren forever to get six

more of the warm rocks into the plane, but when she did she was glad. It was much warmer now, and she crawled in beside Jay. She listened to the wind shake the sides of the plane. She felt like a wild animal, huddled in a dark cave, hiding from the unfriendly wilderness. Her life in Oakland seemed to belong to another world now, and to another young woman. Only that morning, she had been afraid to touch her feet to the cold floor of her apartment. What she wouldn't give to set foot on that floor now!

Lauren's mind flooded with questions that would not let her sleep, no matter how tired she was. Had her friends discovered that she was missing? Did her parents know? Was a search

23

party on the way? Would they find her and Jay in time, even without the flight plan that hadn't been filed? Was the emergency beacon really working, or was it as useless as the radio?

One question crept into her mind again and again. Were she and Jay going to make it through the night? Lauren pushed it out of her mind and wiggled her toes and fingers as if to prove that she was still alive. She wondered how long it would be before the rocks lost their warmth. In the total darkness there was no way of knowing what time it was. Lauren hoped that it was at least three o'clock. Even so, the sun would not be up for hours. With a chill, Lauren realized that the rocks were already cooling off.

"How long until it's light?" Jay moaned, "How long?" In answer, Lauren told him to keep his hands in his pockets and stamp his feet to warm them. She tried to think of warm things: fires, deserts, steaming hot soup. Her stomach growled, and she shifted uncomfortably. Bits of old poems drifted through her mind. Anything to keep her mind off the cold, to keep the fear away. But it was impossible to pretend that the rocks were still warm. Now Lauren began to shiver. She wanted to fall asleep and dream of the sun. But the thought that she might not wake up again kept her from closing her eyes.

Jay's voice pulled her away from her fears. "It's

getting light out there," he was saying. Lauren lifted her head from inside the scarf she had wrapped around herself. She could see that the sky had turned from black to gray.

"We're going to make it! We're going to make it," she said. Over the howling of the wind, Jay's voice answered her. "Yeah, we're going to, we are." Lauren wondered what they would do once the sun was up. She knew that Jay could no longer help himself, now she was responsible for them both.

"Just let the sun come up," she pleaded. "Then the worst will be over."

Every time Lauren looked up from behind her scarf, the sky had changed to still another shade of gray. After a while, though, she peered out of her scarf and saw nothing but white. Not even the mountain could be seen. She sat up to get a better view of the sky. All she could see were the whirling flakes of a blizzard outside the plane. She sank back in despair. Had she and Jay survived that horribly cold night only to be snowed in at daybreak? All at once she heard Jay's panicked voice, and felt the plane shudder.

"I've got to get out of here!" he cried desperately. Lauren watched him get weakly to his knees. His voice was filled with terror. "Help me!" he cried.

"You can't go out there," she yelled. "It won't

do any good." Jay didn't seem to hear her. Lauren thought he was going crazy. He began to beat the sides of the plane with his fists. His voice was on the edge of hysteria. "I can't feel anything," he cried.

Lauren didn't know how to stop him. She pounded on his back with all her strength, but it did no good. She would have to let him be. She squeezed herself into the back of the plane, and buried her head in her arms. When everything was quiet agian, she thought he had come to his senses. All she could hear was the howling of the wind.

Only when she felt the warmth of the sun did Lauren raise her head. She nudged Jay to let him know that they had made it. But when she touched him, his arm felt stiff and cold. With horror, Lauren saw his eyes staring blankly into space. Jay was dead, and now she was alone.

CHAPTER 4

The Middle of Nowhere

Punch, kick, hold. Punch, kick, hold. From an airplane, it would have looked like a tiny spider was inching sideways across the snowy mountain face. But there was no airplane and no spider. Instead, the rising sun warmed the back of a young woman who was scaling the side of one of the highest mountains in the country, wearing only a thin wool skirt, a light pullover, and high-heeled boots.

When Lauren saw the frozen stare of Jay's eyes, she knew that she could depend on no one but herself. Both her friends were dead. There was no search party. She was stuck on top of a mountain peak with no way down. Lauren realized that her only choice—and her only chance—was to make a way. She would have to climb over the edge of the mountain crest again. This time there was no going back.

Lauren studied the slope on the other side of

the ridge when she had climbed back up. She was calm and careful. This time, she noticed there were rocky ledges that stuck out through the snow, all the way down to the rocks below. After that, it seemed it would be an easy climb to the desert floor. She would have to follow the invisible path from ledge to ledge. She could not spend another night on the mountain, huddled next to Jay's body in the crashed plane.

She crept toward the first rock in her path, punching and kicking holes in the ice. Five moves and she made it, hugging the rock and shaking the life back into her numb fingers. Her arms and legs felt strong, in spite of her injuries. Taking a deep breath, she started out for the next ledge. Halfway there, a strong gust of wind shook her. It seemed to blow through all the pores of her body, straight to the bone. She waited to catch her breath, and moved on. As she reached the second rock, she thought to herself, "This is impossible. But I am making it."

Suddenly she heard a tiny rumbling sound in the distance. She looked up to see a plane, but it was much too far away. Lauren realized that it wasn't looking for her or the plane wreck. Punch, kick, hold. She moved on.

After about an hour the angle of the snowfield grew more shallow. Lauren discovered that she could sit down on the ice and slide from rock to

rock. Shoving off, she skidded over to the next one, her heart pounding when she almost missed it. She told herself to be more careful, and looked up to check her progress. The cliff of ice and snow stretched high above her. She had survived the hardest part of her journey.

Lauren let out a shout of excitement that echoed all around her. The rest of the climb would be no problem, she thought, no problem at all. Skidding from rock to rock, she imagined herself running down the rest of the way to the end of the snowfield, as soon as she was able to stand up straight.

When she actually could stand up, though, it was not as easy as she had hoped. With each step, her feet sank into the snow up to her knees, and the snow filled her boots. Luckily her bad leg didn't hurt her, and she was able to keep a steady pace through the snow. The climb down was taking much longer than she had thought, though. And she still had a long way to go before she would reach the end of the snowfield.

As the slope became more level, Lauren was able to go faster, swinging her arms to keep her balance. Now she even found herself looking at the beauty of the wilderness around her. In the morning light, the snow sparkled like diamonds. The rocks seemed to glow. As she moved, Lauren noticed that the colors in her skirt seemed to ripple out in glowing circles. Wonderful patterns began forming in front of her eyes. She enjoyed the vivid colors until she thought that something might be wrong with her eyes. Tired of concentrating on every step she took, she decided to stop for a rest.

Lauren wondered if the sharp glare of the sun and the vast whiteness of the snow had damaged her sight. Was she starting to go snowblind? "Or is it just that I'm tired," she thought. "After all, I've climbed down a mountain with a broken arm and a swollen leg. I've been in a plane crash and watched my friends die." Lauren looked around at the world where she had been dropped, feeling like an unwelcome visitor. As she gazed along the mountain ridge, she saw something that made her eyes open wide. There, straight ahead of her, was a row of charming redwood houses, little mountain homes. And standing on the deck of one of them was a man in a long white robe, his arms outstretched.

Lauren leaped forward with excitement. She headed toward the houses, calling out to the man, "Hello! Can you help me? I've been in a plane crash and I'm hurt! Can you hear?" But the man gave no answer. Just then Lauren lost her balance and fell forward into the snow. Her leg throbbed with pain. When she looked up again, the houses and the man were gone. All she could see was a vast range of rocky peaks.

Lauren blinked, realizing that she had imagined the whole thing. Of course there were no mountain homes up here in the middle of nowhere. She felt disappointed and angry with herself for wasting valuable time. Over two hours had passed since she started out. There was still at least half a mile to go before she would reach the end of the snowfield.

As she continued down the slope, Lauren wondered if her mind was going to play more tricks on her. Firmly, she decided that she would not let it happen again. She was pleased to see that the distance between her and the foot of the mountain was getting shorter with each step. When she saw bits of grass poking through the

ground in the distance, she began to lope through the snow. She couldn't wait to get out of the wet and the cold. The going would be much easier on dry land.

All at once, at the edge of the snowfield, she saw the figure of a man walking towards her with open arms. It was her friend Jim, from Oakland! He must have flown into the mountains with a search party, and they had found her! Now he was here to greet her as she reached the end of her journey through the snow.

Once again, Lauren forced her body to move faster than her tired legs wanted to go. Now, too, she lost her balance on the ice. This time she fell backwards, and skidded the rest of the way to the edge of the snowfield. In front of her was a large rock. She reached out to touch what she thought had been her friend. Of course no one was there.

"OK," she said out loud, picking herself up and brushing the snow off her skirt. "Now I know. If I can touch it, then it's real."

CHAPTER 5

Dream People and a Miracle

Hopping carefully from rock to rock, Lauren made her way toward the streambed which twisted through the canyon below. It wasn't as easy as she thought it would be. She had to be careful not to slip on the jagged rocks. If she broke her ankle in a fall, she would be stranded for sure. Lauren realized that the imaginary people were not the only tricks her mind was playing on her. It also had a way of making her believe that her troubles were over, just as a bunch of new ones were about to begin.

Lauren figured that the dry stream bed would lead her to the desert, she saw that it twisted around many sharp bends and turns, with the mountain ridges rising up on either side. She started to pick her way around the first bend, having no idea how many more would follow. Several times she fell and scraped herself on the rocks. Each time she rounded a bend, she hoped it would be the last one. But the streambed kept twisting and turning, and there was always another bend ahead.

Even though she had been hurt badly in the crash, Lauren felt a steady flow of strength through her body that she could not explain. Every now and then she stopped to rest. She would stretch out on a flat rock and enjoy the warm sun. This way she managed not to get too tired by the climbing. She was beginning to feel more comfortable and safe. It was as if she had become a mountain animal that knew how to take care of itself by instinct. This feeling helped her go on, helped her believe that she would make it safely to the desert.

Lauren began to examine the brush and grass for signs of animal life. She especially hoped to see bits of garbage that people might have left behind. This made her laugh, because she knew that the sight of litter left by careless picnickers usually made her angry.

As she rounded another turn in the streambed, Lauren looked up to see a farmer standing on the hillside above her. She raised her arm to wave, and was about to call out to him when she suddenly stopped herself. She knew that this was another one of her "dream" people, and she ignored the urge to go up and talk to him.

There was nothing but rock all around her as

she made her way down the streambed. The
bends came one after another, slowing her down.
But she had no choice, there was no other way to
go. On a ledge above her, she saw a woman with
a sketchbook, painting wildflowers. "Another
phantom," Lauren told herself. She turned her
eyes back to the rocks at her feet. Even though
she felt that any moment she would come upon a
ranch or some people who could help her,
Lauren told herself that she must not stop to
investigate. "Unless they call out to you," she
ordered herself, "you have to ignore them."

By this time the streambed had become thick
with sagebrush. It tore at Lauren's skirt and legs.
"Soon," she thought, "soon I'll get to the end of
this path. Soon I'll round the last bend. Maybe
this is the last one." Lauren made her way
around the corner of another rock. Suddenly she
found herself standing at the edge of a dry

waterfall that dropped a hundred feet to the canyon below.

"Oh, no!" she cried. She felt trapped. There was no pathway down, just a sheer drop to the floor of the canyon. But she couldn't turn back, and she couldn't stop either.

As she had done at the top of the mountain, Lauren closely studied the drop. She saw that there was a series of narrow ledges all the way down. As before, she could climb from ledge to ledge. This time, though, it was all rock. She tried not to think of what would happen to her if she lost her hold on the rock and fell. In her mind, she went over the rules she had learned when climbing in the hills with her friends. Test for strong handholds and footholds. Keep your feet close together. Keep your stomach flat against the rock.

She took off her boots and dropped them onto the first ledge, which was fifteen feet below. Then, her heart beating fast, she lowered herself over the side. Carefully she edged her way down, clinging to the rocks. She could not make a single mistake now. Every move had to be perfect.

When her toes touched the ledge, she felt a mixture of relief and fear. She had started a dangerous climb that she would have to finish. She concentrated all of her energy on every tiny hole in the rock that her fingers and toes found.

The climbing went well as long as she thought of nothing but each rock, each step, each hold.

On one ledge she found a natural ladder to the ledge below. A long treetrunk had fallen and lodged itself between the two. Lauren tested it. She was happy to find that it was strong enough to hold her. Quickly she climbed down the trunk and found an even better surprise waiting for her below.

The ledge she reached now was about fifteen feet wide. In the middle of it was a sunlit mountain pool of melted snow. Taking off her clothes, Lauren climbed down and slid into the pool. She let the cool water wash away the blood and grime and sweat. For a few moments, she felt like she was in paradise. Then she climbed onto the dry rocks nearby, and stretched out in the sun.

She was startled to feel the eyes of another human being upon her. Embarrassed, Lauren was pulling her clothes on when she saw a man hanging out from the wall of rock across from her, about fifty feet away. She blinked and he was gone. But in his place was a row of houses with yards, lawn furniture, even two parked cars. This could not be a vision. Lauren cut across the gorge and began to climb the slope toward the houses. Now she could see a man on his front porch. She heard the slam of a screen door. Reaching out, she touched rock. The phantoms vanished from sight.

Trembling, Lauren turned back and made her way across the gorge. Her confidence was shaken by the tricks her mind was playing, especially since she had promised herself that she would not be fooled again.

At the bottom of the last ledge was a deep pocket of snow. Climbing over the side, she let herself fall backwards into the drift. Lying on her back, she could see the wall of rock and granite she had just scaled. Lauren knew that it was a miracle she had survived.

CHAPTER 6

We've Been Looking for You

As the sun moved overhead, Lauren trudged over the rocky terrain. Now she was using a stick she had found to help her along the way. She saw still more of the mountain phantoms her mind created. But she was determined to stick to her course, and she ignored them all. The sun was still warm, but the shadows cast by the mountain ridge grew deeper. Lauren guessed that she had only a few hours of sunlight left. She was beginning to feel weak, but she would not let up. "I will not cry," she told herself. "I must keep on."

When she joined up with the streambed once again, she was pleased to discover that it was now filled with sparkling water. By this time her shredded boots were flapping about her feet as she walked. So she decided to leave them behind and walk barefoot through the water. At first, traveling this way was a nice change, and the water felt good to her feet. After slipping on the rocks and falling into the water a few times, however, she grew tired and impatient. But each time she immediately got up and went on, grumbling about the pain of another new bruise.

The sound of the rushing stream grew stronger and louder until it became a giant roar. Lauren found herself perched on the edge of a magnificent waterfall. Climbing through the spray, she made her way up a sandy hill that rose to the left side of the falls. On the other side was a slope that led down to the desert floor. She stood at the top of the hill for a moment, hoping that she could believe her eyes. There were no more cliffs or mountain peaks, no more waterfalls, no more ledges or jagged rocks. Only this one last hill. Lauren managed to tumble down the last few feet of it. A little landslide of gravel came along with her as she landed at the bottom. She got to her feet and quickly found the path of the stream again. Following it for a while, she noticed out of the corner of her eye what looked like a marked trail. At first she thought it was another trick her mind might be playing. So she peered closer, as the waters of the stream rushed about her swollen feet. There, in the middle of the trail, was a dried pile of horse manure. Still not ready to trust her eyes, she walked slowly over to the mound and kicked it with her foot.

"It's the real thing!" she shouted, her eyes

filling with tears. To Lauren it seemed the most beautiful thing she had ever seen in her life. It meant that help was nearby.

She started down the sandy trail, each step hurting her raw and bloody feet. The canyon she was walking through widened into an open valley. She found a sign posted on a tree, and she felt the carved letters with her fingers to make sure that the words were really there. It said INYO NATIONAL FOREST ZOOLOGICAL AREA. She didn't recognize the name of the forest, but that didn't matter.

After a while, she came upon two parked cars, real cars. She knew when she saw the reflection of her scratched and grimy face in a sideview mirror that they were real. But she decided not to wait for the owners to return from their camping trip. She wanted to find the highway, and get a ride into town. Above all, she wanted to find a place where she could wash, and call her parents and lie down on a clean, soft bed.

Now that she was so close, her exhaustion threatened to take over completely. Twilight fell over the valley. Now Lauren spotted the twinkling lights of the city up ahead, and the highway that led to it.

As she walked, Lauren wondered what she would say to the first person she met. She knew anyone would be startled by her appearance. Would they believe her if she told them she had been in a plane crash at the top of the Sierras? That she had climbed over cliffs and waterfalls? That she had made it all the way down the mountain on her own?

The sun dropped at last behind the mountains. Lauren reached the edge of the highway just as darkness fell over the valley. She saw a car approaching, and waved her hands over her head for it to stop. The car sped past her, though, without even slowing down. She knew she must look awful, and stumbled down the highway toward the lights of the town. Her head was spinning, and her feet were burning with open sores.

Lauren headed straight for a flashing sign that said "Motel." Through the window of the office, she could see the glow of a television set. She rang the doorbell, and tried to think of what she would say. The young man who opened the door took one look at her and opened his eyes wide with surprise.

She started out slowly, trying not to slur her words. "I've been in an accident. A plane crash. Do you have someplace I could rest?" Glaring, the young man shook his head. "Sorry, can't help you. We're full up," he told her. Lauren watched the door close in her face.

"Well, at least he's real," she sighed as she turned away. Had she come this far to have doors closed in her face? Would she have to spend the night sleeping in the open?

She went over to a pickup truck and leaned in, about to tell the driver her story. There was no one inside, though, and she crept off down the street. "I don't know how much longer I can last," she thought.

Across from her she saw an old fashioned hotel, THE WINNEDUMAH. She climbed the steps to the porch and crossed the creaking wooden boards to the entrance. The lobby was furnished with some old sofas and a piano, and had a musty smell to it. Trying hard not to stumble on her weak legs, Lauren came up to the desk. The old man behind it was reading a newspaper. When he saw her he put it down and looked at her unsurely.

Lauren used her last drop of strength to speak.

"Is . . . is there a phone?" The words came out in a whisper, her voice gone.

Behind her a door flew open, and two men came in. "That's her!" one of them said to the other. He was the young man she had talked to at the motel. The other man was the sheriff, and he caught her by the arm. Was she going to be arrested?

"Is your name Elder?" he asked. His voice was not angry, but gentle and kind. Lauren nodded yes, unable to speak. The sheriff smiled. Then he said the words Lauren had been waiting to hear. She would remember them for the rest of her life.

"We've been looking for you, dear. Let me help you."